➤► FABER CLASSICS ◄◄

FABER & FABER

has published children's books since 1929. Some of our very first publications included Old Possum's Book of Practical Cats by T. S. Eliot starring the now world famous Macavity, and The Iron Man by Ted Hughes. Our catalogue at the time said that 'it is by reading such books that children learn the difference between the shoddy and the genuine'. We still believe in the power of reading to transform children's lives.

About the Author

Ted Hughes (1930-1998) was born in Yorkshire. His first book, *The Hawk in the Rain*, was published in 1957 by Faber & Faber and was followed by many volumes of poetry and prose for adults and children. He received the Whitbread Book of the Year for two consecutive years for his last published collections of poetry. He was Poet Laureate from 1984, and in 1998 he was appointed to the Order of Merit.

About the Illustrator

Joe McLaren is a freelance illustrator. He graduated from the University of Brighton in 2003, and now lives and works in Rochester, Kent. He has taught Foundation Illustration at Central Saint Martins, and has worked on internal and cover illustrations for a number of publishers.

The Tigerboy

The Tigerboy

TED HUGHES
Illustrated by JOE MCLAREN

First published in The Storyteller (second collection) in 1979
by Ward Lock Educational Co Limited
This edition first published in 2016
by Faber & Faber Limited
Bloomsbury House, 74–77 Great Russell Street
London, WC1B 3DA

Typeset in Plantin by M Rules
Printed and bound by
CPI Group (UK) Ltd, Croydon, CR0 4YY
A CIP record for this book is available from the British Library
ISBN 978-0-571-32062-2

2 4 6 8 10 9 7 5 3 1

There was a boy.

Nothing peculiar about him. His name was ordinary too, Fred. Nobody noticed him. In his gang of friends, he looked just like the others. At home, where he was the middle of a family of five children, he mixed in unnoticeably with the rest. He ate whatever was given.

Only Fred knew he was different. As he went about, doing what everybody else did, he had this idea all the time that he was different. He was special.

But he never did anything different. He slept in a room with his two brothers. He had the same toys as them. They had rabbits and he had a rabbit. They sailed boats and he

1

sailed a boat. They made model aeroplanes and so did he. When his elder brother brought in comics, they all read them. When his brothers went fishing, he went with them and caught fish. When they went to the woods he went to the woods. When they went to school he went to school.

Only at night sometimes he lay awake after they'd gone to sleep. How was it he was here, in this strange thing of a body, that ended at his toes and his fingers and his hair? What had happened to him before he came? Why was he only himself, and not somebody else? He lay awake thinking about this. How was it he was himself, inside this funny skin? How was it, among all the millions and millions of people there was only one of him, and he was it? And he would lie there, clasping and unclasping his hands slowly and thinking, So this is me! And he would whisper, This is you, Fred.

Then one night it began.

His left foot began to itch. He scratched. The more he scratched the more it itched. 'I've got a flea,' he thought. But it wasn't just one place, one bite. It was all over his foot equally, above and below, and right up to his ankle-bone.

After a while his foot was so sore with scratching he had to stop. He seemed to have got the upper hand of the itching for a while, and he went to sleep.

Then he had a dream.

In this dream he was of all things a goat. Everything was dark and he was a very frightened goat. He was a goat wanting to bound away. But a rope round his neck held him tethered. At first he couldn't see anything, but gradually as if his eyes were growing used to the darkness he began to make out branches above and stars, then the post he was tethered to. He was in the middle of some sort of clearing among trees.

And as he saw all this he saw something dreadful. A lumpish black shape was moving and he knew, he absolutely knew, it was something dreadful that was going to jump

on him. He let out a wild screeching bleat –
but he was too late, the shape was in the air,
then he was crushed by its weight.

After that a number of things happened
at once. A dazzling light flooded everything
and he saw the massive striped arms of the
giant beast that was bundling him up. Its jaws
closed round his back and he knew he was
being picked up. At the same time a sudden
bang deafened him. Then he was flashing
through darkness, twigs and leaves lashing
him as he went, and with a mighty effort he
came awake.

He was stumbling among scattered toys
in his darkened bedroom, while his brothers
shouted to him.

When everything was sorted out, and his father had been in to settle them down, it turned out that his eldest brother had heard him uttering the most ghastly bleating cries. He had switched on the light and managed to get a glimpse of Fred fighting out of his bedclothes when the lightbulb burst with a bang and everything went dark. In the darkness Fred had scrambled into the far corner of the room. What a nightmare!

But long after his two brothers had gone to sleep again Fred lay wondering what had happened. Did the tiger escape with the goat? Had it carried him off into the jungle and eaten him? Had the hunter with the torch managed to wound the tiger with his shot?

What happens to a goat that gets eaten by a tiger?

As he thought these thoughts Fred felt his left foot beginning to itch again. He reached down to scratch it and almost jumped out of bed with fright. He felt again more carefully.

Then he climbed quietly out of bed and quietly opened the door. The light on the stairs was always left on for his baby sister, and it showed him quite clearly all he wanted to see, as he put his left foot out onto the landing.

Just as it had felt to be! His left foot was covered with fur. But what horrified him most of all was that it was thick, yellow fur.

He was too frightened to wake his parents. Too frightened to wake his brothers.

He crept back into bed and closed his eyes tight, praying to God to make his foot ordinary again. And so he fell asleep.

In the morning he was wakened by his brothers telling him of all the racket he had made in the night. As if he couldn't remember it! The whole thing came back to him as if it had been waiting at the side of his bed.

Very cautiously he felt for his left foot. He almost cried with relief. It was smooth, human and normal. His own foot had come back!

That day was a schoolday. In the bustle of the morning, he forgot about his dream. Then it was arithmetic first. He enjoyed school because he had invented a way of handling his lessons. One day he had been daydreaming, his chin in his hand, his head screwed round, his gaze directed up into the sky through the topmost classroom window, when the maths teacher's voice had burst in his ears like a bomb.

The blackboard was covered with figures and the teacher was staring at him alone.

'I said what are you dreaming about, Willox?'

Fred stared. The class sat in hushed fear. The teacher, who was tall, bony,

with fierce black eyebrows and a savage sarcastic temper, looked as if he might attack any second.

'Tell us what you were dreaming. Was it something inspiring? It must have been something.'

Then, to his own horror, Fred heard himself saying:

'I was an eskimo, sir. And I'd killed a great whale, and me and my dogs had dragged it out on the ice and I was skinning it with my walrus-tooth knife.'

The maths teacher put back his head and laughed a false, big-toothed laugh like a jackass. Then his fierce eyebrows came back. And he spoke in an icy voice:

'In future, Willox, in my lessons, you are permitted to dream of one thing and one thing only.'

'Yes, sir.'

'Do you know what that thing is?'

'No, sir.'

'You can dream you are Einstein, a genius mathematician. And instead of a whale you will kindly drag this very real Universe of ours out onto the ice, do you hear that Willox? For me. And you will skin this Universe with numbers alone, Willox, never mind your walrus-tooth knives. You have only one tool in my lessons, Willox, and that tool is number, the most razor-sharp instrument ever invented by man.'

Fred stared, feeling stupid. The class sat silent, trying to make something of what their explosive teacher had just said. The teacher smirked and went on with the lesson.

But Fred was thinking 'skinning the Universe with numbers'. That phrase kept coming back and it gave him a weird thrill. 'Skinning the Universe with numbers!' When they started doing their maths exercises Fred invented a funny voice, which he thought would be like a genius mathematician's, and he invented imaginary spectacles and an imaginary potty look, and started doing his sums.

To his amazement, he could suddenly do them like magic.

And they were all correct.

After that, in maths he always imagined he was this potty mathematical genius, who was designing a spacecraft at home which would be driven not by fuel but by working out intricate maths problems. You just stuck a huge maths problem in the fuel slot, everything would begin to whirr, and the rocket would be off. When the answer shot out, you had to have another problem ready. You just fed in the problems and all the business of the computers working them out was what drove the rocket.

And as long as he imagined he was this potty genius his maths lessons were strangely easy. Not only that, they were exciting.

The maths teacher began to treat him with favour, so he soon had an important job in Fred's rocket system, which was spreading its stations right through the galaxy. He had to think up problems that would take a rocket exactly to its destination without refuelling. He sat in a tiny room, and simply invented problems.

Fred had bigger things to think about. His rockets could now dematerialise and rematerialise in any one of twelve other dimensions. It was all done by mathematics. Each dimension was full of strange beings and events and laws.

But it wasn't just maths. He discovered the same method worked for science and physics.

In those he was the genius inventor, with mad eyes, brother to the genius mathematician, and supplied all the gadgets and weapons needed in his rocket conquest of the twelve dimensions of the Universe.

In geography he was a tireless explorer, with skinny steely legs and a brick-red face and pale eyes and a very posh voice, cousin to the inventor and the mathematician, and for history he simply switched his whole rocket system into a thirteenth time-travel dimension.

So on this day with all this he forgot about his dream of the tiger until the end of the day, and then in the last lesson the English teacher read them a story about of all things a man-eating tiger. A tiger in India had killed over a hundred people, one by one, and eaten them. Now the hunter set out to kill it. As he listened, Fred sat in growing fear. The hunter bought cows and staked them out in the jungle at likely points, and on the first night the tiger killed one, and ate half. Then the hunter built a platform in a nearby tree and sat over the half-eaten cow with his rifle, which had a powerful torch lashed alongside it. But that night the tiger didn't come back to the cow as the hunter expected. Instead it broke into a hut over ten miles away and dragged out a woman and disappeared with her. So the hunter followed the blood-trail and at last found the remains of the woman in a gulley. Then though it was a terrible thing not to take away the remains and bury them, the hunter sat up a tree over the poor woman's head and arms and legs until night fell.

Night came suddenly. Warning calls came from the jungle creatures. Fred listened in terror. He was listening for the tiger. And the tiger came. The hunter heard a long low sigh, and stared down into the pitch darkness. He levelled his rifle slowly and aimed towards the sound, then switched on the torch. At that moment Fred shouted at the top of his voice:

'Look out!'

The whole class, which had been listening in tense silence, jumped and turned round.

The teacher stopped reading. All eyes were fixed on Fred.

'What in the Lord's name is the matter with you, Willox? Are you all right?'

'Yes, sir.'

'Then what are you shouting at?'

'It was the tiger sir.'

'What, were you trying to warn it or something?'

'Yes, sir.'

The class tittered, the teacher called for silence and read on. The hunter saw the tiger in the light of the torch and fired. With a crashing roar the tiger leaped away into the darkness. Had he hit it? What had happened? Just then the bell rang for the end of lessons and the whole class groaned.

Fred ran all the way home, every now and then making great leaps, thinking about the tiger.

When they were all in their beds and the light out, Fred started to tell his brothers the story of the hunter and the tiger. They listened in dead silence. He told it very slowly, putting in all sorts of details, because he wanted to frighten them. Finally he got to the point where the hunter was sitting in the tree, over the grisly head and arms and legs of the woman, with the stump of dead branch sticking into his ribs and his legs gone dead and the jungle night falling. Then the terrible silence. Then the deer barking its tiger warning half a mile away. Then an even worse silence. And at that point – when he knew the tiger had arrived in that pitch darkness, and he was just about to tell about the strange, low sigh, Fred's whole body froze. To his surprise, he found he couldn't speak. Tears of fear were pouring down over his ears into the pillow.

After a few moments one of his brothers said:

'Go on then, what next?'

Fred lay silent. He simply could not utter a sound.

'He's gone to sleep,' said another voice.

The tiger's eaten him,' said the first. But nothing came from Fred. The two brothers sank off to sleep.

And Fred too, who lay not daring to move, finally drifted off to sleep.

He was standing under a tree. It was pitch dark but gradually he made out that it was the laburnum tree at their garden gate. His eyes adjusted rapidly. He saw the empty street quite clearly, all the sleeping house fronts, as if the moon had come out. But it wasn't the moon. He realised he could see in the dark. The next thing he realised was that he was a tiger.

His first thought was that he must get away from the front of the house as quickly as possible, because if his mother looked out and saw him she would be frightened. Also,

if anybody else saw him from some other bedroom they might guess where he'd come from and start enquiries.

He leaped over the garden gate with a wonderful sensation. It was such a joyful feeling, he went bounding up the middle of the street, like a giant, silent spring.

Suddenly, inside one of the houses a dog started barking madly. He imagined its goggling eyes and bristling neck.

Immediately Fred was away. He kept in close to the garden walls, so anybody looking out would most likely miss him. He took the shortest cut to the open country.

He had no idea what he was going to do. He felt restless, full of seething energy. He thought he might just run a few miles. So long as he didn't meet anybody. It never occurred to him to worry what might happen at dawn.

It was such a wonderful feeling, being a tiger, that once he got beyond the last houses he raced through the darkness, which to him was as clear as if he had headlights. He only wanted to run all night, leaping over the cattle and horses.

A strong smell of cows, a hot green cud-chewing smell, came to him. Twirling up his long tail, he bounded towards the dark shapes of cattle lying in a huddled bunch. Gleefully, he thought what a fright he would give them. A roar seemed to gather itself at the bottom of his chest, but he kept silent. He didn't want to wake the farms with the unnatural roar of a tiger. He permitted himself a few grunts, marvellous booming sounds, as if he had a big drum in his belly, as he loped across the grass. He would leapfrog over the whole lot.

Then in mid-career he stopped, flattened to the grass. He had seen two things. One was a big animal, nearly twice the size of a cow, that had got up from among the cows and was enlarging towards him, giving loud sniffs and snorts. It stopped and began stroking the ground, as if it were trying to wipe something off its forehoofs. A bull! And that bull seemed to know all about the smell of tiger.

But that wasn't all. Another animal, away over to the left, was suddenly even more interesting than the bull. It was so interesting that Fred actually forgot about the bull for a moment, and stood up, to get a clearer view.

Standing on the far side of the field, looking at him, was another tiger.

But then the ground was shaking and the bull was coming. Fred felt no fear. He considered leaping over it, leaping aside, or meeting it head-on with a blow of his paw, which felt strong enough to knock a tree down, and he was thinking that when he'd got the bull out of the way, he'd go and investigate that other tiger.

But while he stood trying to decide what to do if the bull hit him. He would never have believed anything could be so heavy or so hard. He knew it was too late to think of doing anything. He was already flying through the air, numbed with the awful black shock of the bull's impact.

He landed on the floor at the side of his bed. Wildly, before anybody could put on the light, he felt at his face and ears. He was normal. He sat there for a while, beside the bed, letting the ordinary world come back.

The rest of that night he did not sleep. He kept his eyes as wide open as he could. He was afraid of both the bull and the tiger, waiting there for him the moment he closed his eyes. He didn't feel like sleeping either. Now and again he would reach down to feel his foot, to see if the fur had come back.

Next day was a Saturday and no school. He idled away the morning with his brothers, polishing their bicycles for the Sunday ride. But at last he left them and rode off to the edge of town. He rode along the cinder path by the canal, he left his bicycle in the grass, climbed a fence and crossed a field. Even before he got to the thick hawthorn hedge he paused. From the field beyond came a dreadful sound. For the first moments he was certain it must be a tiger, maybe that other tiger. It was a groaning roaring complaining sound – like somebody roaring down a long pipe. He crept to the hedge and peered through. There were the black and white cows. And there was the bull. A big white bull. He was walking through the herd, here and there pawing up sods and flinging them back over his haunches, lifting his nose to sniff and make that terrible sound. He was so thick and white and huge, he looked like some other species than the cows.

Fred retreated. His adventure as a tiger had given him a whole new notion of the world of bulls. He had never properly looked at one before, but now he had seen enough.

He got back home as fast as he could.

But an odd thing happened when he reached home. He saw his aunt's red car drawn up at the front gate and felt a little jump of pleasure, knowing that her dog Peter would be with her. This black labrador was a particular friend of Fred's. Whenever they met the dog would go into a frenzy of joy, writhing and squirming towards him, making gleeful whimperings, nearly hurling itself from one side to the other with the violent swings of its tail, and lifting its upper lip from its teeth in a dog laugh and standing up to embrace him.

Fred ran into the house. His brothers were there with two friends, all going round on hands and knees, pretending to be dogs fighting, and Peter was taking part in frenzied delight, growling and barking and whacking the furniture with his tail.

As Fred came into the room he called to Peter, 'Here boy!', to get him away from his brothers. The dog jumped up erect and looked at Fred, tail swinging. But after that first look a strange transformation took place. Peter's body seemed to double in size, as all his black hair stood on end, and all his teeth appeared as his face shrivelled up in a mad snarl, and he backed away crouching. Then suddenly he uttered a yell, and dashed from the room into the kitchen, yelling as if he had been run over.

Fred's mother came out of the kitchen demanding to know who'd hurt the dog. His brothers stood up, baffled. Fred could hear his aunt in there, coaxing Peter.

'Something's absolutely terrified this dog. I can't get him out,' she called. Then they all went into the kitchen. His aunt was on her hands and knees, reaching under the stove where Peter had jammed himself far back against the wall.

Fred bent down, eager to reassure his friend, and reached a hand under the stove. 'Come on, Petie boy,' he kept saying, 'come on.'

A noisy scramble turned into a black silent bolt of dog hurtling from the

kitchen back into the living-room. Then everybody heard a crash of glass, followed by silence.

They went into the living-room and saw the jagged edges of the main front window. Peter had obviously gone straight through.

The boys rushed outside. Peter had disappeared. The boys started to hunt.

But Fred didn't join the hunt. His meeting with Peter had frightened him afresh, more than it had frightened Peter. He knew that what had frightened Peter was a tiger.

Somehow, looking at his old friend Fred, Peter had seen a tiger.

Fred went to his bedroom. He took his shoes off and felt his feet, then sat looking into his eyes in the mirror. After a while, even though it was early afternoon, he crept under the blankets. What should he do? Ought he to tell somebody? What if he actually was turning into a tiger?

He just didn't know what to do. And he didn't dare tell anybody. He found a book and lay there, trying to read.

When bedtime came, Saturday night, his brothers were noisy, but Fred told them he had a headache and lay in bed with his face turned to the wall.

Gradually they fell silent. And Fred, too, eventually sank off to sleep.

THE END

If you enjoyed

The Tigerboy

why not read more

Faber Children's Classics . . .

⤜ THE FABER CLASSICS LIBRARY ⤛

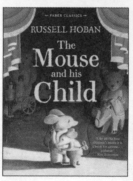

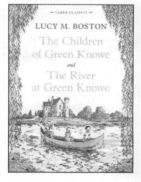

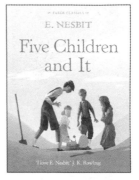

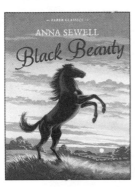